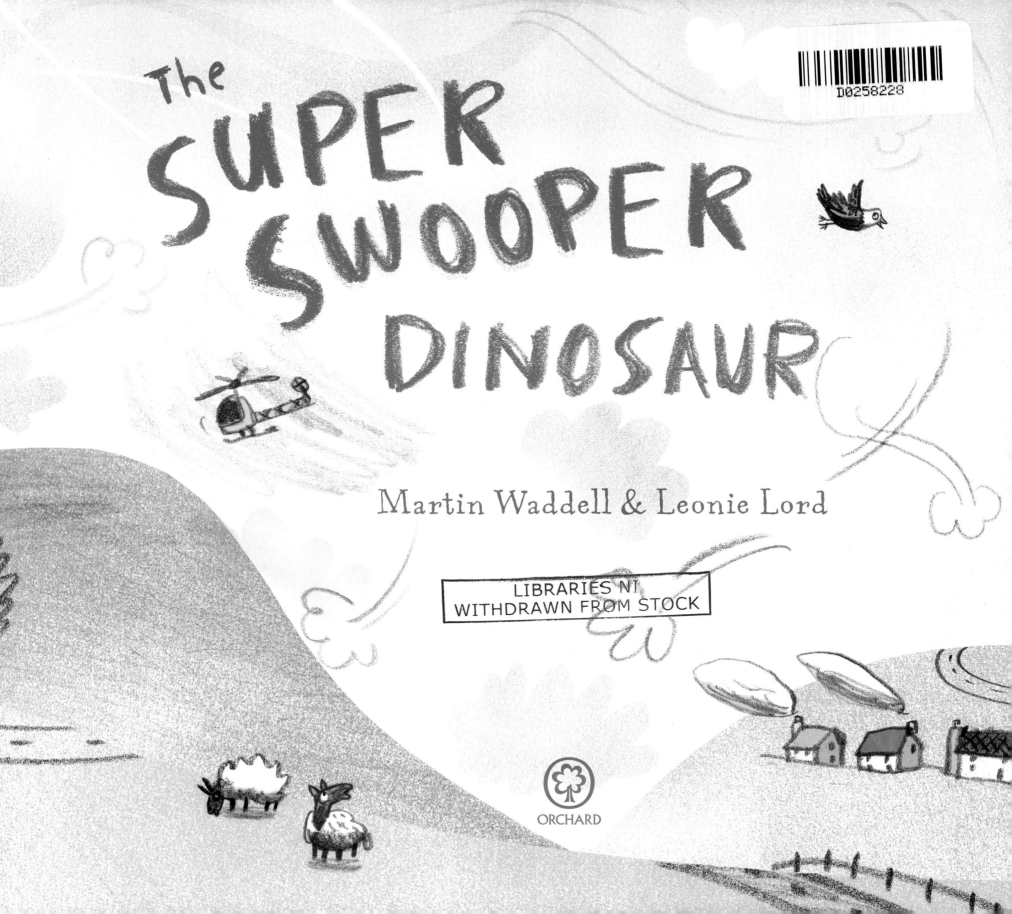

The SUPER SWOOPER DINOSAUR

Martin Waddell & Leonie Lord

ORCHARD

One day, Hal and his little dog, Billy, were out playing when the sky darkened and . . .

A SUPER SWOOPER DINOSAUR

landed in Hal's garden.

KER-PLUMP!

"Can I play with you?" he asked Hal and Billy.

"Yes, please!" said Hal. "What games will we play?"

"Hide-and-seek!" suggested the super swooper.

So, they played hide-and-seek.
The super swooper was so excited he
got himself into a flap!

100!

99...

98...

"Here I come . . ." called Hal.

"Maybe you're a bit too big for hide-and-seek," said Hal.

"Perhaps we should try something else," Hal suggested.

"How about dino dancing?"
said the super swooper.

"Just copy me – I'm an ace dino dancer!" said the super swooper.

Stomp Stomp Stomp

diddle dee diddle

The super swooper swooped up onto the roof of Hal's house and danced on the tiles.

"You can't dino dance on the roof!" said Hal.

Hal had to do something, so . . .

"Last one in the paddling pool is a BLUE BANANA!" shouted Hal.

Hal raced outside but . . .

"Look out below!"
cried the super swooper,
swooping down towards the
paddling pool.

SPLASH

Hal's mum got
SOAKED!

"Oh, Mum! We're so sorry!" said Hal.
But Hal's mum was cross. "Your games are too rough and rowdy," she scolded the super swooper. "If you can't play nicely with Hal, you'd better go home!"

The super swooper was VERY upset.
His bottom lip wibbled and wobbled and he started to sob.

"Please, Mum, let him stay. We're his best friends," said Hal.

"He has no one to play with but us. COME ON, MUM, PLEASE?" pleaded Hal.

"Oh, all right . . . he can stay,"
said Hal's mum.

"Thank you so much!" said the super swooper.

Then the super swooper flapped his wings to get Mum dry.
"Thank you very much!" said Hal's mum.

And she went to get cool drinks on a tray.
"What will we play now, Hal?"
the super swooper asked.

"Hide-and-seek didn't work, dino dancing was a disaster and the paddling pool was a big, BIG mistake," sighed the super swooper.

"I know what we'll do," said Hal.
"We'll do what you do best of all!"
So . . .

. . . they swooped and they swooped!
(Which is what super swooper dinosaurs do when
they're having fun with their friends.)
And it was the best game EVER!